W9-ART-203

A Pipkin of Pepper

Copyright © 2005 by Helen Cooper
All rights reserved
First published in Great Britain by Doubleday, an imprint
of Random House Children's Books
Printed in China
First American edition, 2005
1 3 5 7 9 10 8 6 4 2

www.fsgkidsbooks.com

Library of Congress Cataloging-in-Publication Data
Cooper, Helen (Helen F.)
  A pipkin of pepper / story and pictures by Helen Cooper.—1st American ed.
    p. cm.
  Summary: While making pumpkin soup, three friends discover they have no
salt and go to the city to buy some, but while Cat and Squirrel head straight to
the salt store, Duck pauses at a pepper shop, then fears he will never see his
friends again.
  ISBN-13: 978-0-374-35953-9
  ISBN-10: 0-374-35953-9
  [1. Ducks—Fiction.   2. Cats—Fiction.   3. Squirrels—Fiction.   4. Missing
children—Fiction.   5. City and town life—Fiction.]   I. Title.

PZ7.C78555 Pi 2005
[E]—dc22
                                                                    2004060003

FOR
ANNIE EATON

A Pipkin of Pepper

Helen Cooper

Farrar Straus Giroux
New York

S omething was bubbling in the old white cabin.
What was in the cooking pot?

Pumpkin Soup!

Made by a Cat, a Squirrel, and a Duck,
waiting just for a pipkin of salt
to make it the best you ever tasted . . .

but . . .

"There's no salt left!" quacked the Duck.
They'd run *clean* out,
it was true.
There wasn't a grain, not a speckle of salt,
to put into the Pumpkin Soup!
Would it still be the best you ever tasted?

NO!

The Cat said, "I'm going shopping."

"Oh, please," begged the Duck. "Let me come, too."

But the Duck hadn't been to the City before,
and he had a habit of wandering off.

"What if you get lost?" the Cat mewed.
"I won't!" squawked the Duck. "And if I do, I'll tell a Police Dog."

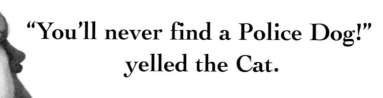

"You'll never find a Police Dog!"
yelled the Cat.

"If you're ever lost," said the Squirrel,
"the best thing to do
is stay where you are, and we'll find you."
"Better yet, don't get lost at all,"
said the Cat.

I t was time to catch the bus.
"Can I go?" pleaded the Duck. "Can I go?" he said,

and he wiggled,

and wheedled,

and bobbed,

and begged,

until the Cat said, "All right!

If you promise to hold on tight."

"And I'll come, too,"
said the Squirrel,
"and hold on to *you*."

But the Duck felt scared
when he first saw the City.
It was very big,
and very busy.
He stared at the stores,
and the towers,
and quacked,
"Let's buy that salt
and go straight back."

"Hold on tight," said the Squirrel.
"The salt shop isn't far from here."

And the Cat led them past
more towers,
and more stores,
selling all sorts of things:
puddings and pastries,
pilchards and prawns,
lobsters and lightbulbs,
pizza . . .

. . . and pepper . . .

And that gave the Duck a clever idea.

"Wouldn't it be fine," he murmured,
"if we bought some pepper
for the Pumpkin Soup.

I bet it would taste . . .

. . . delicious!"
he quacked.
"Can we buy some pepper?"

"Pepper?" squeaked the Squirrel.
"We won't need that."

"There's the salt shop," said the Cat.
"We have a job to do, and we don't
want to miss the bus back."

The PEPPER POT

A PIPKIN OF PEPPER FOR THE PUMPKIN SOUP!

Muntok White
Malabar Pepper
Pink Pepper
Green Pepper
Royal Pepper
Cracked Pepper
Black Pepper
Red Pepper
Chili Pepper
Sweet Pepper
Hawaiian Rainbow Pepper
Cayenne Pepper
Jalapeño Pepper
White Pepper
Pimiento

But the Duck wasn't even listening.
He was thinking about pepper, for the Pumpkin Soup.
"Would one pipkin be quite enough?" he turned around to ask . . .

but . . .

. . . the others had gone!

"Lost!"

quacked the Duck.
"I'm lost in the City!"
He scuttled off, in a terrible tizzy.

Inside the salt shop,
the Cat and the Squirrel
were busily buying
a small bag of salt.
They didn't even notice
that the Duck was missing,
until the salt
was paid for and packed.

"Where can he be?" howled the Cat.
And the Squirrel wailed,
"Where did we see him last?"

"At the pepper shop!"

they shouted together.

They hurried back.

But the poor Duck
was lost in the crowd.
 He couldn't even find
the pepper shop now.
He collided with a kind Mother Hen.

"Are you lost?" she clucked.

"Yes!" bawled the Duck.
"And I can't find my friends."

"Where did you see them last?" asked the Hen.

"At the pepper shop," sniffed the Duck.
"And I should have waited there
till they came back . . .

but I forgot."

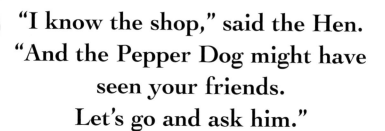

"I know the shop," said the Hen.
"And the Pepper Dog might have
seen your friends.
Let's go and ask him."

I HOPE CAT AND SQUIRREL STAY IN ONE PLACE

"A Cat and a Squirrel?" said the Pepper Dog.
"They just left by the other door."

"I'll never see them again!"
wailed the Duck.

And nothing would cheer him up.

Not even a drink,

not even a snack,

not even a packet of pepper.

"Hush," said the Hen.
"We've dialed 911.
Any minute now, they'll come right through that door."
Pretty soon . . . through that door . . .
came

six Police Dogs, with megaphones,

four helpful Fire Dogs,

two Foxes,   who left rather quickly,

and . . .

AT LAST . . .

the Squirrel and the Cat! The Duck was so pleased to see them.
The Cat wasn't cross, and the Squirrel didn't scold,
even though they'd missed the last bus.

"Who needs a bus?" quacked the Duck.
"We've got a Police Dog to fly us home!"

The Cat and the Squirrel were happy.
They had their salt for the Pumpkin Soup.
As for the Duck, he had his packet of pepper.
He held it tightly all the way back.

Home again, in the old white cabin.
Pumpkin Soup in the cooking pot.

Made by the Cat who slices up the pumpkin,
made by the Squirrel who stirs in the water,
made by the Duck who tips in a pipkin of salt . . . and . . .

 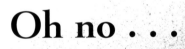 

a pipkin of pepper.

Oh no . . .

a packet of pepper!

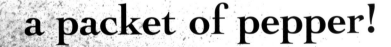

Would the soup still be

the best you ever tasted?